# Ballerina Swan

by ALLEGRA KENT

*illustrated by*

EMILY ARNOLD McCULLY

SCHOLASTIC INC.

# Glossary

*barre* [bar]: A handrail used for support during exercises.

*épaulement* [ay-pohl-MAHN]: Elegantly positioning the shoulders so that one is forward and the other is back with the head turned or inclined.

*grand jeté* [grahnd jeh-TAY]: A high jump from one foot to the other, this step looks like a split leap.

*plié* [plee-AY]: Bending the knees; often a warm-up exercise.

*port de bras* [pour duh brah]: A movement in which arms pass gracefully through several positions.

*For my granddaughters, Miranda Alice and Georgia Iris;*
*for my agent, Faith Hamlin; and in loving memory of*
*George Balanchine, who understood unusual casting*
—A. K.

*For Allegra*
—E. A. M.

ISBN 978-0-545-54100-8

Text copyright © 2012 by Allegra Kent.
Illustrations copyright © 2012 by Emily Arnold McCully. All rights reserved.
Published by Scholastic Inc., 557 Broadway, New York, NY 10012, by arrangement with Holiday House, Inc.
SCHOLASTIC and associated logos are trademarks and/or registered trademarks of Scholastic Inc.

12 11 10 9 8 7 6 5 4 3 2 1          13 14 15 16 17 18/0

Printed in the U.S.A.          40

This edition first printing, January 2013

The text typeface is Golden Cockerel.
The artwork was created with pen and ink and watercolors.

𝓕ROM HER POND IN A CITY, Sophie loved to watch
the dancers in Madam Myrtle's Dance Studio. She saw
them bend and stretch and stand on their toes. She
saw them spin and turn and leap.

One day Sophie flew to the window ledge for a better look.
The children stopped dancing and went to get a better look too.

"Back to your *barre*," Madam Myrtle commanded.

Sophie quickly flew back to the pond.

The next time Sophie went to look, she hid in the corner.

But Sophie couldn't just watch. She had to dance too.
One day she gathered her courage and entered the building.
Beautiful music drifted through the door.

Hoping not to be noticed, she crept inside and joined the dancers in their exercises—a series of *pliés*.

But she was indeed noticed. Madam Myrtle shouted "SHOO!" in the most frightening way. Sophie, her lovely neck bowed in shame, withdrew from the room.

But the humiliating episode couldn't quell Sophie's love of dance.

One day Madam Myrtle didn't appear for class. In her place was a young woman who looked very much like Madam Myrtle but was younger and way jollier.

The dancers all looked jollier too. And they danced lighter and higher than ever before.

The music and dancing were irresistible. Sophie decided to try to take class once again.

When the new teacher discovered the swan in her studio,
Sophie braced herself for what she thought would be coming.

But the unexpected happened. The teacher, whose name was Miss Willow, ignored that Sophie was feathered, webbed, and winged, and treated Sophie like all her other students. She even gave Sophie a helpful correction.

"You are going to have to work on your turnout," she said.

When it came time for *grand jeté*, Miss Willow said, "Fly,
my children!" The children jumped as high as they could,
but only Sophie could really fly.

"That was very good," Miss Willow said to her.

After that Sophie went to class
every day. She learned that some
things came very easily to her, and
other things were difficult.

Because of her long, graceful neck, she
was very good at *épaulement*. But as she had wings instead of arms,
*port de bras* was a challenge. Because of her webbed feet, Sophie had
to work extra hard on turnout. But she was very good at *grand jeté*.

One day Miss Willow said, "I am impressed by your commitment and hard work. I would like you to audition for our end-of-year performance of *Swan Lake*."

So many emotions flooded through Sophie's avian heart: joy, hope, and fear—Sophie's heart would break if she was not cast.

When the day of the audition came, Madam Myrtle joined
Miss Willow at the studio. A new person entered the room. The
choreographer, Mr. Balletski, demonstrated each combination,

which the children and the swan were required to imitate. Some of the combinations were easy and familiar. But some were very, very hard.

At last the time came for the roles to be announced. All the dancers were eager and fearful. Sophie was most eager and fearful of all. As she scanned the list, she didn't see her name. She read the list more carefully. Still she didn't see her name.

# CAST LIST

**Princesses**—*Gayle, Linda, Nina, Mary, Trista, Joanna, Barbara, Susannah*

**Friends**—*Bret, Desmond, Marshall, Gary, Henley, Eric, Bruce, Chip*

**Swan Maidens**—*Pam, Cassandra, Jessica, Lindsey, Ruby, Wendy, Marijka*

**Palace Guests**—*Emily, Liz, Judith, Franco, Robert, Suzy, Bob, Roger*

**Masters of Ceremonies**—*Jacques, Clinton*

**Dramaturge**—*Grace*

**Von Rothbart**—*Marcelo*

**Prince**—*Danil*

**Odette**—*Tallulah*

**Odile**—*Flora*

**REHEARSAL**
Monday
3:00
*All cast
members*

Sophie walked off in deep shame and disappointment. She bowed her head low so no one would see her tears.

But someone did. It was Madam Myrtle.
"Why are you crying?" she asked. "Aren't you happy
with your role?"

Sophie looked up. Her role? "Your name is on the back of the
list," Madam said. "Didn't you see it? Mr. Balletski created a part
just for you. You will be the swan."

For weeks Sophie practiced and practiced and practiced. She attended every rehearsal—even rehearsals in which she didn't have a part. And when she wasn't practicing, she listened to her music and pictured her steps in her mind.

On the day of the performance, Sophie was ready.